This book is dedicated to my daughter Rogue Arya Dutra. You're my favorite ever.

SUICIDE ERRANDS

BY
GEORGE DUTRA

CHAPTER 1
MIKE

Most love stories have a happy ending. Mine does not.

I'm Mike and I have what most people consider a great life. But this isn't about how great my life is. It's about how much I can't fucking stand it or the world we live in nowadays. I have a easy, high paying job at a very nice restaurant. But I cant stand it there. It's just a bunch of stuck up assholes spending a ton of money on food they don't appreciate, brought to them by people they don't respect. My girlfriend is a beautiful personal trainer that is actually kinda funny and on paper is just about perfect. Except for the fact that I'm pretty sure she's fucking someone at her gym. Actually I think it's more than one. I have a nice apartment downtown that most people would kill to live in. But I can't stand it there either. There's a few people, and I do mean a few, that are cool. So that's like 3 people out of a whole building that aren't pieces of shit. I mean people leave trash in the hallways. Rarely pick up their dog shit. And someone stole my Christmas wreath one year! I pay almost 3 grand a month to live there. You'd think this type of stuff wouldn't happen. It just feels like people don't care about each other. Maybe they never did.

    Lastly we have my family. This is a real special group of assholes. Especially Alice. That's my mom, but I don't call her that. She hasn't earned the right to be called mom or mother. She's a horrible person. Durning my grandmothers (dads side of the family) funeral she actually called me while I was at the service to ask me what my stepmom was wearing and if she looked fat. DURNING THE SERVICE! When I hung up on her she texted me to send her pictures of my step moms dress. She also used to get drunk and hit on my friends once I was old enough to go to bars. No joke, she would just show up to a bar I was at, most of the time already hammered and hit on my friends. It just made everyone super uncomfortable.

My dad is no better. All he cares about is himself. He just drinks and gambles. My brother passed away and he's just never been the same. In fact my parents got divorced right after it happened. Since then he's pretty much stuck to himself. My sister has 2 sons, 5 & 7 and he's only seen them 2 times. Imagine living in the same county as your family and never seeing them. The only one he talks to is the one that will give him money or rides to the bar, which is me. The only one I will actually miss is my sister. Considering who raised her she's pretty cool. She's a great mom to my nephews and is a good person.

The only thing only thing that gives me any pleasure is the gym. I've been doing MMA for about 20 years now. Since high school. When I'm there and I'm training it's the only time the chatter in my head stops. It's the only time the stress goes away. I'm even happy when I'm the one getting beat up. Getting punched in the face or choked out is about as real as it gets. But unfortunately its the ONLY real thing I have in my life. Everything else is just filler. I thought about becoming professional fighter but at the time I just wasn't good enough and now I'm too old. I'm just sick of pretending like I give a fuck about any of it. My job, my apartment, my girlfriend, my family.

But I'm mostly sick of my life and the world we live in. I'm sick of doing the same shit, day after day. Wake up, workout, go to work, see my girlfriend, go home. It's always the same thing I did yesterday and the day before that and the day before that and the day before FUCK!!! I'm done. I'm sick of all this mundane repetitive bullshit, that in the end doesn't mean anything. When it REALLY comes down to it, does it really matter what kind of towels I have? What kind of shoes I wear? What kind of car I drive? No. It doesn't mean shit. But we all act like it does. We take pictures of our food like it really matters. 800 million people in the world are starving and we're talking pictures of our food like we're at a goddamn museum. I'm so sick of humans. People make me want to not be here anymore. Their selfish. They lie. They hurt you. And the worst part is most of the time they don't even feel bad about doing it.

So I'm done. I'm gonna kill myself.

But I have a super fucked up case of OCD or whatever bullshit I have in my head. So I can't just kill myself. I have to get all of my affairs in order. I have to take care of my apartments lease and rent. I have to take my clothes to The Goodwill. I have a letter to my sister I need to drop off. Then I gotta go to the bank and close my account. And believe me, I know you're probably asking yourself "why the hell does he care about any of that shit? He's killing himself." Well you just said it. I'm killing myself. So I think its safe to say logic went out the window a long time ago. No of this makes sense. I'm just telling you what happened. Oh yeah, one more thing I forgot to mention. Today is my birthday. I turn 40 today. I figured why not end it on the same day it started. If anything it'll make for a cool hedge stone. Here lays Mike Braggton 4/14/1975 - 2015.

CHAPTER 2
SUMMER

After breakfast I headed out to get started on my suicide errands. That's pretty funny. Suicide Errands. I hope they put that in the paper when they announce my death. "He spent his last day doing his suicide errands". Before anything I needed to get gas and what happened next would change things forever. Isn't that what they say in books and movies? Change things forever? As I pulled into the gas station a woman walked right in front of me, forcing me to slam on my breaks to avoid plowing into her. She swung her arms in the air making the contents in her over sized bag fly everywhere.

"WHAT THE FUCK ASSHOLE!" She yelled and slammed a open hand on the hood on my Bronco. I jumped out of to help her pick up all the her shit that flew out of her bag. I say shit because she really did have the most random things in her bag. Papers. Like crumbled up papers. A makeup bag. 2 water bottles. But what was the most alarming is the amount of pill bottles she had. There were at-least 12-15 of them. When she noticed me notice them, she picked up her pace a bit. "You could have fucking killed me." she said.

"I know. I really am sorry." She grabbed the 4 pill bottles I had picked up from my hands and shoved them in her bag. "Well keep your eyes on the road fuck-face." We both stood up and I answered her with "Actually it was a parking lot, I was already off the road." As soon as it left my mouth I knew I fucked up. "Are you fucking retarded or something? Watch the fuck out for people." Before I could answer her she walked off towards the bus stop and sat down on the bench. I walked back to my Bronco and finished pulling into the station and next to the pump. I got out, started the pump and went inside to get something to drink. I grabbed a Yerba Mate and got in line. I could see her through the store window. I couldn't take my eyes off her. She was without a doubt the weirdest, most beautiful creature I'd ever seen. She had long blonde dreads that were all the same size and looked like they were very well maintained. Which was weird because the rest of her looked so not maintained. She had some of them in a ponytail and some just going wherever. Her shoes were the most torn up, worn out pair of Vans I had ever seen. And I lived in California, where Vans are pretty much a required part of the dress code. Her dress was this long flowing thing that looked like it used to be on a flamenco dancer in Spain.

    Her dress was so long all I could see of her socks was that they were white and that was through the holes in her shoes. She also had on a Sex Pistols shirt on that looked so old it could have been on Sid Vicious when he died. But the best part of her outfit was her sweater. She had on one of those old man sweaters, the kind with patches on the elbows. Like some snobby college professor. This chick was a mess. But her face. WOW. She was so strikingly pretty. Blue eyes that somehow looked white when you looked up close at them. Her nose was the perfect balance between big & small. Her mouth looked like it could sing or whistle or do something musical.

    After paying for my drink I walked to my Bronco and returned the nozzle back to the pump. I jumped in and just sat there for a second watching her. Suddenly the bus pulled up and she began to get on board. I started up the Bronco thinking she was gone. But after a few seconds and an exchange of words, it was clear she didn't have enough money to get on the bus. She stepped off yelling at the bus driver and gave him the middle finger before she went to sit back on the bench.

I couldn't tell you what was drawing me to this girl. But once the bus drove off leaving her behind, I couldn't stop myself from pulling up next to her. I rolled my window down and asked "Excuse me, I feel really bad about almost hitting you. Can I give you a ride somewhere?". She just sat there, no change of expression. No response. "Listen I understand if you don't want to. I just wanted to at least offer." I started to roll up my window and then she asked "What are you doing today?". I was thrown off by her question but I answered "I'm just running a few errands."

    She got up from the bench and walked to the passenger side window and leaned her forearms on the door. For the first time I could see her arms were covered in tattoos. "Turn on your radio." she said. "My radio?" I asked. "Yeah, your fucking radio. I'm not getting in if you're listening to some country bullshit or some other fag music." Was this chick for real? Who talks like that? But the despite the way she asked, I turned up the music and the sounds of the street faded away. The Vandals must have been ok because the next thing I knew she was climbing into the passenger seat.

    "My name is Summer." She said as she buckled up. "Nice to meet you Summer, I'm Mike." I don't know why but I was really nervous with her in my Bronco. "Where can I take you?" I asked her. She just sat there looking out the window. Finally after a few seconds she asked "So what's your first errand?" completely ignored my question. "I'm on my way to The Goodwill." She got excited. "I live the Goodwill." Pointing to the bags in the backseat. "Is this what your donating? That's a lot of clothes to give away. What's wrong with them?" She asked. "Nothing." I answered.

"Then why are you getting rid of them? Did you used to be a fat fuck?" I laughed a little. "No. Just giving them away." Before I was done answering her, she was turned around going through one of the bags. She gave me a look that said she didn't believe me. "Why is that so weird? I have plenty of clothes." I know I sounded odd. My voice went up a little and I felt like I was panicking. But I didn't know what else to say. I wasn't expecting to be asked questions about going to the Goodwill. Also I couldn't tell her I was getting rid of this stuff because I'm killing myself.

    She pulled out a sweater and held it up to her chest to see if it might fit her. "This is a fucking Burberry sweater. It's at least $300, maybe $400 bucks! And you're just giving it away?" How the did she know how much it cost? It was actually a little bit more than $400. Most of the clothes were pretty expensive. But fuck it. Let someone else enjoy them. "I just don't want any of this stuff anymore." I told her. "Well I'm taking this sweater." She said has she stuffed it into her already full bag.

    "So once The Goodwill hits the lottery with all this shit what else do you got to do today? You giving this Bronco away" She asked me. I don't know why I was telling her anything, but there was a certain part of me that was glad to be talking to someone today. To not spend my last day alone. "I have to go to my bank, my landlords office and just a couple other things. What about you? What do you got going on?" I don't know why I asked her that. She obviously didn't have anything to do if she jumped in a complete strangers car. She looked at me with a sly smile and said "I'm taking a me day." I gave her a smile back and said "Fair enough. I could use the company." She pointed to my phone and asked "Do you mind if I change the music?". I shook my head no. She grabbed my phone and started looking through it. The next thing I heard was Gigantic by the Pixies. What a great first musical impression to make. For the rest of the drive we didn't talk very much. She just sat there lightly singing the words. It was barely audible, like a singing whisper. Like she was almost shy. But Summer was anything but shy. I tried not to stare at her while I was driving, but fuck it was hard not to. She was such an interesting person. Summer was the type of person you wanted to get to know purely out of curiosity. It was just her dumb luck she was extremely beautiful too.

CHAPTER 3
THE GOODWILL

We pulled into the Goodwill parking lot and I turned the engine off. I looked at Summer and said "I'm just gonna run right in real quick and drop off these bags." Leave the keys so I can listen to the radio. She could see tat the thought of me leaving the keys made me very uncomfortable. "Uh I ..". "You don't have to worry. I'm not going to steal you ride." We both stared at each other for a second. Neither one speaking. "Fine! Just hurry the fuck up. I'll just sit here like a fucking dog. Good thing the top is down." "I'll be right back. I'm just dropping these off". I said putting the keys in my pocket. I wasn't leaving them with her. No way. I started to walk away and heard Summer say "Hurry the fuck up then." I was beginning to rethink giving Summer a ride. I walked across the parking lot and into the Goodwill. Once inside I threw the bags on the counter. "Excuse me!". I turned around to see who I was annoying this time. It was an old Mexican lady. She was in the front of a pretty long line of people. All of them holding bags just like mine. "There's a line buddy." Said the woman as she pointed to the back of the line. I turned to the kid behind the counter to pled my case. "Excuse me, I just want to donate these." He didn't even look up to answer me. "Well thats the line" I looked out the store window to check on Summer. I could imagine her turning into a puppy and chewing my seats up. I looked back to the kid and said "Why do I need to get in line, I'm just dropping these off?" Finally the kid stopped ringing up his customers items and looked at Mr before he said "Dude if you want cash or store credit for this stuff you gotta get in line." I didn't understand. "I don't want either, I just want to donate this stuff. Give it away." Now the kid didn't understand. "So you don't want the money or store credit?" Then out of nowhere I heard the horn from the Bronco blasting, Everyone in the store looked outside and saw what I saw. Summer was standing outside the drivers side door with her arm in the window and hand on the horn. She had a cigarette in her other hand the she was puffing away on. Then everyone looked at me. Then when I shrugged and gave a embarrassed grin, we all looked back at Summer. Who still had her hand on the horn. I threw the bags at the feet of the old lady "They're all yours." Then I walked out to the Bronco and stood about 2 feet away from Summer. I really thought once I came outside she would stop honking the damn horn. But she didn't. We just stood there staring at each other With the horn blasting. And what I thought was a cigarette was actually a joint. I just want to take a second to appreciate this scene. So we have a guy thats trying to get some things done so he can go home and kill himself standing in a parking lot with a crazy homeless looking woman smoking a joint while she's honking his horn. WHAT THE FUCK IS GOING ON HERE? I cant have this shit going on right now. Fuck this I thought. I reached out and grabbed the joint from Summers mouth. She didn't even flinch. She also kept her hand on the horn. It was pretty hard but I didn't let her crazy commitment get to me. I took the joint a took a long drag off it. I blew the smoke in her face and calmly said "Summer get your fucking hand off my horn". She took her hand off the horn hand grabbed her joint back and said "Ready to go to the bank?" Then she walked around to the passenger side and got in. I just stood there for a second or 2. Why didn't I just tell her that I can't have her with me? Then I thought 'who cares, I'm not going to be here tomorrow'. I got behind the wheel and grabbed my phone and but on some music. Deftones. It didn't hit me until we drove off that the name of the song was My Own Summer (Shove it).

CHAPTER 3
THE BANK

We got to the bank before the song was over. I pulled into the parking space and turned the engine off. I looked over at Summer. "Your not staying in the truck this time are you?" I asked her. She didn't answer me, she just got out, walked around to my side and opened the door. "After you my sire." She said in a pretty good English accent while she bowed. I just got out and followed her towards the bank. Once we got in I noticed Bill Shipman at his desk. Bill has been my accountant and managed my money since high school. He also handled me sisters finances.

But the truth is he just kisses my ass because I make a bunch of money and never spend it. And just like everything else I can't stand how fake Bill is. Summer and I make our way towards his office. He noticed us and got up from his desk to meet us in the doorway of his office. "Mikey, how goes it? Everything OK?" Bill said has he pulled out a seat for Summer to sit down. I sat in the chair next to her and said "Yeah Bill, I'm fine. I just have a few things I need you to do." "Well you name it buddy and you got it." Bill said as he sat back down behind his desk and started typing on his computer. "Let me just pull up your file."

Summer grabbed a caramel from the bowl on Bills desk and then put the wrapper back in the bowl. Bill just smiled at her and took the empty wrapper from the bowl and put it in the trash can under his desk. "Ok Mike, what can I do for you? You got another stock you want to buy shares in?" Bill asked. "No not today. I'm actually going to close my accounts." I could see confusion first on his face and then pain and then him pull himself together all in matter of seconds. Man, he was good. I bet he killed at poker. Finally he asked "Are you moving? We have branches all over the country." "I'm not moving Bill." I told him. "Is it the ATM fees? I know you mentioned them before. They're gone no more ATM fees." "Bill its not that. Look, I assure you its not anything the bank has done. I just wanna close my accounts and I don't really want to say more than that." Bill looked at me and then to Summer who gave him a huge smile and a shrug of her shoulders and then back to me before saying "Mike I know we just have a professional relationship, but 16 years is a long time to have any type of relationship. Shit man, you went to my divorce party. So I'm inclined to ask one more time if everything is ok." I looked at Summer before answering him. She was such a put together mess. And now that I was up close to her I could see that she was even more beautiful than I had thought. She gave me a different smile than the fake one she gave Bill. It was the smile you'd give someone that was in on a joke with you. I don't think she meant it to effect me the way it did, but there was something in her smile that gave me strength. It was like she was saying 'if I can dress the way I want, talk the way I want, then you can kill yourself the way you want.' Of course this was all in my twisted mind and I'm sure it was just me having a crush on her that was effecting my judgment. But nonetheless her smile made me feel better about was I was doing. "Everything is fine Bill." I assured him. He could tell that I wasn't going to change my mind and he let out a big sigh and said "Well how do you want to handle this, do you want me to transfer funds to your new account." Bill was acting like he was being broken up with, fishing for information about his ex's new flame. "Bill I'm not cheating on you with another bank, I promise." I told him. Summer laughed. I took a pen and a post it note from his desk and wrote a few numbers down and passed it to him. "I want the first and second amounts each on a money order. The 3rd number is what I want put into my sisters account. She still banks here right?" He nodded. " OK good. I'll take whatever's left in cash. It should be about $530 bucks." Bill took a deep breath, looked at Summer, then back to me and then put both hands on his desk before standing up to reach out his hand to shake. "We're sorry to lose you business Mike. I'll go get those money orders." I told him "Thanks Bill, I appreciate everything you've done to help me over the years." "It was my pleasure. I'll be right back." Bill walked out of his office towards the tellers. "Dude he was about to fucking cry." Summer said once he was away." I couldn't help but laugh out loud. She leaned over closer to me and looked me in the eye. "Alright, what the fuck is going on? You gave away all your clothes. You closed your bank accounts. I would say you're on the run from the cops or the mob, but you're way too square for that shit." We just met. How did she know what I was too square for? "How do you know I'm not on the run?" I asked her.

 "Are you?" "No, but I could be." She laughed and said " Look I'm just saying you seem too smart to get mixed up in some dumb shit." She just looked at me a little longer. Then she snapped her fingers and said "Cancer!" Just then Bill walked back into his office with the money orders. Summer and I both stood up from our chairs. Bill handed me the money orders and then the cash. "Here ya go, 2 money orders and $542.34 in cash." I took everything from him and shook his hand. "Bill I can't stress enough that this has nothing to do with you or the bank. You have both been good to me over the years." Bill reached out to me with both arms and gave me a big hug. I looked at Summer who made a circle with one hand and sticking her finger from her other hand in and out of the circle to make the point that Bill and I were fucking. Finally Bill let go and I pulled away. "Fuck George, the truth is you've made me a ton of money over the years. You were a great client and I wish you the best."

Then Bill let out a huge breath and his whole posture changed. He went from a tall thin guy to a shorter guy with a beer gut. "Dude! What the fuck was that?" Summer said exactly what I was thinking. "Have you been holding your gut in this whole time?" I know Mike is a workout freak. So I just keep it (slapping his belly) sucked in when he comes in. Ya gotta relate to your clients." Summer laughed out aloud and then we all had a good laugh. "Bill I like it. High-five buddy" Summer said and bill gave her a high-five I shook Bills hand one more time and we walked out of his office. Once we were outside Summer said "Bill is fucking crazy." I agreed and opened her door for her. "Do you always open doors for girls?" she asked. "Yeah, most of the time. Why?" I asked. 'It cute and all but I'm a big girl. Plus there might be times when we're more like a team than a couple." I walked around to my side and climbed in. "Like what if we go on a beer run, are you going to open my door then or are we just gonna jump in this bitch and bail?" I had to admit she made some fucked up sense. "You make a good point. How about if when we leave banks or liquor stores you let yourself in?" I told her. She said "Throw in any crime scene and you got a deal." We shook on it.

CHAPTER 4
THE LANDLORD

"So where next Captain?" Summer asked. "My landlord." She turned up the music. This time it was Bob Marley, Memphis. Summer definitely knew good music. We drove to my landlords pretty much in silence. I had a lot of shit I have always wanted to say to him. He's a total scumbag. He had an office in Anaheim. My building in Newport Beach was his nicest property. Most of his properties were run down buildings in Orange County. The guy was a slumlord for sure. When we finally got to his office I said "Things might get a little heated in here." Summer looked and me with a serious face and then pulled a knife out of her bag. "What the fuck Summer?!" I asked. "What? You just said its gonna get heated." "Just put it back, put it back." Summer put it back into her bag and we both got out and walked to the building. Before I opened the door I said "Just let me do the talking." Summer saluted me and said "Yes sir."

    I opened the door and we both walked in. The front area of the office was dark and the furniture was from the 70's. There was a old couch with stains and a few cigarette burns, a filing cabinet and a desk. The windows had the curtains drawn and didn't let any sunlight in. Amanda the secretary was at her desk on her phone and didn't even bother looking up. "Just drop your rent in the box." Amanda said pointing to the envelope box along the wall." Amanda was a pretty college dropout thats been here about a year. We chat a little when I drop on my rent each month. "Hey Amanda." She looked up from her phone. "Mikey! How are you?" She said excitedly putting her phone down. Then she noticed Summer and her excitement disappeared.

"I'm good. Is Carl in?" I asked. I knew he was, I saw his piece of shit Caddie out front. "Yeah, let me tell him your here." Before she could reach the intercom I was already at his office door. "Mike! What the fuck is this bullshit? You don't fucking knock? And who the fuck is this chick?" Carl spit out in between bites of buffalo chicken wings from what looked like a family size bucket. Carl totally had the classic slumlord look. Bald, fat, short, smoker, he had it all. Looked like fucking Danny Devito. This guy was a fucking pig and I hated him. I sat in one of the chairs. They didn't match. None of the furniture in Carls office matched. I'm sure it was just stuff left by different tenants over the years that he kept for himself.

"Did you fucking hear me asshole? Who the fuck is she? Amanda why the fuck did you let them in?" Carl yelled. Amanda was in the doorway panicking and didn't know what to do. This was totally out of my character. But she knew I hated Carl and that I made sure to drop off my rent when I knew he wasn't in his office. "She didn't. I let myself in." I told him. Summer was still standing behind me by the door. "Summer shut the door." I said. Summer pushed Amanda back outside of the office. Amanda just backed out staring at Summer in disbelief at what was happening. Summer just smiled at her while slowly closing the door on Amanda.

I knew that Carl had been a landlord for a long time. So I was pretty sure he'd seen and had to deal with a lot crazy shit. Carl just sat there and grabbed 2 more wings out of the bucket, threw one in his mouth and put the other on the plate in front of him. Once he finished eating it he wiped his mouth with a towel and said "Well asshole you wanna tell me what the the fuck you're doing here or is your girlfriend here gonna give me a lap dance?" Then he pulled the bones from the wing out of his mouth and shoved the other one in. "You fucking wish I was here for that you fat fuck." Summer said. Carl laughed, spitting out a little sauce. "I like her." Then he spit the bones from that wing out on to the plate and wiped his mouth. I looked at him and said "I'm here to let you know I'm moving." He leaned back and threw the towel on his desk and pulled a cigar out of his shirt pocket and lit it then asked "Why? Didn't you just renew a couple months ago?" "No, I'm supposed to renew in a few months."

"Why you trying to get out with only 3 months left. Just fucking wait. You've been there like 8 years. What's 3 more months?" Carl asked. "I cant. I'm moving." I answered. "Where to?" He asked me. "It doesn't matter. I'm not renewing in 3 months." I told him. Carl leaned back in his chair and looked back and forth between me and Summer before saying "You didn't need to come in here to tell me that. You know you could have just emailed or called. So why the theatrics, what the fuck is this really about?" "I'm here to pay my rent for the next 3 months." I said as I threw a money order on his desk. "This is the next 3 months minus my security deposit."

Carl took a long drag off his cigar and said "How do I know you'd get your security deposit back?" "You don't" I answered him. Carl looked at Summer for a long time and without looking away he said to me "Anything else or is that it?" He said still looking at Summer smoking his cigar. "Yeah, there is." I said as I got up and went to his side of the desk, grabbed the cigar out of his mouth and put it out on his desk. "You fucking asshole!" Carl yelled and then tried to get up from his seat. From where I was standing it was easy for me to grab his wrist and the back of his neck and slam his face on his desk while twisting his wrist back behind him to leverage him to stay down.

As if she had done something like this before, Summer locked the door. "You better fucking let me go you piece of shit! Do you know who the fuck I! AAAAAA!!". I gave his arm a pretty good twist to let him know I was serious. "OK OK OK. Stop please." Carl pleaded with me. "Carl shut the fuck up. You are a piece of shit slumlord." I told him. "What the fuck do you know? You live in fucking Newport Beach". I gave his arm another twist. "OK OK OK. Wait". "Are you done?" I asked him.

"Yeah" he grunted back. "Good. There's a woman in your building on Dale & La Plama in Buena Park, Mrs. Fromm. She's in apartment 217". I told him. He tried to turn his head to talk "What about her?" He asked. "You're going to stop raising her rent every 3 months and you're going to fix all the shit in her apartment that she's been trying to get you to fix. The heat, the lights outside, the water are all fucked up there and she's been trying to get you to fix them for over a year." "What the fuck do you" I pushed on Carls head.

"Alright I'll do it". I let go of him and walked back to the other side of the desk. Carl was grabbing his shoulder. I threw the other money order on his desk. "This is her rent for the next 12 months." Carl grabbed the money order forgetting about his shoulder. He let out a audible gasp at the money order. "Once this runs out you're going to start charging her what you did when she moved in. Tell her you lowered her rent since she's such a good tenant." Carl looked like he wanted to say something but didn't. "You're also not going to cash her rent checks for the next 12 months." I added. Carl looked confused and then asked "Why is she going to give me rent checks if you just paid her rent for the next year?". I looked him in the eyes and said "Because you're not going to tell her I paid it."

Carl thought for a second before he asked "So you just want me to collect her rent checks and not cash them? What the fuck am I supposed to do with them?" "Throw them in the shredder. Burn them, rip them up. I don't care, just make them uncashable." I turned to Summer and said " Get Amanda in here." Summer unlocked the door and called Amanda into the office. Amanda walked in and covered her eyes. "Amanda what are you doing?" I asked her. "Do you have a gun? I don't want to see it if you do." Summer made a gun with her hand and shot Amanda in the head about 5 times.

Carl spoke up "He doesn't have a gun you fucking idiot.Uncover your eyes for fucks sake." Amanda took her hands down and looked around the room. I turned to Carl and said "Do I need to come back behind the desk?"Carl straighten up "No, stay there." "Then don't talk to her that way." I told him. I turned back to Amanda "You ok?" She nodded. "Good." I said and then turned to Carl. "Tell Amanda what she is supposed to do with Mrs. Fromms rent check for the next 12 months." Carl took a deep breath and then very quietly said "Put them in the shredder." "What am I supposed to do?" she asked. "Put them in them shredder I said!" He yelled back.

"The shredder? But why?" Amanda asked. "Don't worry about why, just do it." He snapped back. "OK." I turned to Amanda and said "Thanks Amanda. You can go back to your desk." Once Amanda was out of the room Summer shut the door behind her. I turned to Carl and said "So we're clear here right?" Carl lit his cigarette and took a hit and then said "Yeah we're clear." "And just so you don't get any ideas I'll be keeping track of Mrs' Fromms account and if I see anything I don't like I'll be back to have another meeting." Carl waved his hand and said "Yeah yeah, I get it. We're good. I don't give a fuck who pays her rent as long as it's paid." I stood up and Summer opened the door. "Hey." Carl said. Summer and I stopped in the doorway. "What?" I asked. "What do I do if the old lady kicks the bucket before the 12 months is up?" He asked me. I hadn't thought of that. "Well, I guess you get to keep what's left." That definitely changed his shitty frown to a thin smile. As we walked past Amandas desk she looked up from her phone and smiled. "See you later Amanda" I said before I stopped to lean down and whisper something into her ear.

Than I gave her a small kiss on her cheek. "Bye Matty" She said sadly waving as Summer and I walked back out into the sunlight instantly putting my hand up to block the brightness. "So what did you whisper to her?" Summer asked once we were in the Bronco. "What?" I heard her, but I just didn't want to tell her. "You fucking heard me. What did you say to her?" I started the Bronco. "Why? What does it matter?" Summer turned the engine off and said "I don't know what the fuck is going on. Your clothes, your bank accounts, now you're assaulting your landlord. Why do you have me riding around with you?" I looked at her with confusion and said "Are you serious?

I offered to give you a ride wherever you wanted to go. You're the one that asked what I was doing." I snapped back. Summer took a breathe and said "Look all I'm saying is this seems like a lot of serious personal shit. So I'm just gonna go." With that she got out of the Bronco. The thing is I didn't want her to go. I didn't know it till just then but having her there made this a little easier. I got out and chased after her. "Summer wait, at least let me give you a ride somewhere." I stood in front of her. She just looked at me for few seconds and then finally said "Tell me what you told Amanda."

"What? What do you care what I told her?" I said. Summer just looked at me waiting for me to tell her what I said to Amanda. I threw up my hands and said "Fine, I told her not to give up on school." "Really?" Summer asked. "Yeah really. The reason she's working with Carl was to learn more about real estate because she was going to school to be a lawyer that dealt with properties and tenants rights." Summer's face changed from bitchy to warm. Then she said "That's actually pretty cool. Good for her." Then she got in the Bronco like nothing happened. What was I doing? I couldn't keep her around. I had to go to my sisters next. I got in the Bronco and sat there thinking of the right thing to say. "I think it might be time for me to drop you off. Where do you want to go?" She looked hurt and honestly I think a little sad. "Because I asked you a question?" She asked.

"No I just have more stuff to do and I don't know, don't you think it's a little strange driving around with me?" I said. "I can't go home." Summer said quietly. "What do you mean you can't go home yet?" I asked. Summer took a deep breathe and rubbed her face in her hands. "I'm in a sober living house for women. I'm supposed to be out until 5 looking for a job. So I can't go back yet." I looked at my watch. Shit, it was only 12:30. Great now I was stuck with her another 4 hours. "I mean I don't even know you or anything about you other than you live in a sober living house." I said. "Well I don't know anything about you except a bunch of weird shit. I. Mean what the fuck is really going on? Why did you take me a long with you? I didn't fucking ask you for a ride. YOU came up to me remember?" I nodded. "And now you want to ditch me. Fine asshole just take me back to the fucking gas station. The sober living house is right around the corner." She said.

Damn it, she was right. I was trying to ditch her. But I also liked having her around. Maybe she helped me keep my mind off the fact that I was gonna kill myself. I know I had a plan and all that. But the truth is I was scared. So far I was just running errands. Suicide errands. But when the time came would I have the guts to actually do it? Fuck it, why do I care if she's with me. It's just a few more hours. "I have to go to my sisters. If you wanna still hang out you can come with me." I told her. Summer asked "Can I drive?" "Do you even have a license?" I asked. Summer looked pissed "Why you dick? because I live in a sober living house?" She said. "Yeah, thats exactly why." I answered. Summer just let out a huge laugh. I joined her. I started the Bronco and pulled out of the parking lot with Hatebreed coming through the speakers.

CHAPTER 5
MY SISTERS HOUSE

We pulled up along the curb of my sisters house in Costa Mesa. My sister was a child psychologist but she works for the county so she makes shit. But her husband makes good money so they had a pretty nice place. We got out of the Bronco and I grabbed the guitar case that was under the blanket in the back. "That's been there the whole time?" Summer asked. "Yep" I said as I pulled it out of the Bronco. Summer looked at the case and said "Gibson, nice. What year?". Most girls wouldn't ask a question like that. She could tell I was surprised by her question and said "What? I can't know about guitars because I'm chick?". "No, I just". "Just what?"

She snapped back. But I didn't have anything. "Your right, I did say that because you're a girl. I'm sorry. It's a 1962 sunburst." Summer didn't hide her thoughts and let me know "Are you fucking kidding me!? You've been driving around with a 1962 Gibson in the back of you Bronco that has no shell?" "Yeah" I said. "The whole time we were in the bank? She asked. "Yeah" I said. "The fucking landlord?" She asked "Summer its been there the whole time. So yes, wherever we went it was there." She shook her head and started walking towards the house. "You're a fucking idiot." I followed her up the Salk walk into the front yard. "You're probably right." I said.

When we got to the porch I picked up the fake rock in the plant and pulled out the key. I handed the guitar to Summer and out the key in the lock. But before I turned it I turned to Summer and said "My sister is super anal about her place, so please don't touch anything. It's like a museum." Summer whispered "apple don't fall far from the tree." I stopped to look at her. You realize for that saying to work my sister would have to be my daughter." Summer pushed us into the house and said

'Whatever, your in the same family is the point. Same tree. You're just as anal as your sister." She laughed out loud and I did my best not to. "I'm sorry, I'm sure your sisters into anal way more than you are." I lead us to the kitchen. I set the guitar on the table and grabbed a note pad and a pen from your counter. I pulled out a chair and sat to write a note.

    Before I could stop her Summer was eating out of a box of Captn' Crunch. "So who gets the Gibson?" She asked me. "My nephew Carter." I told her. "That's cool, how old is he?" "11" I answered. She walked over to the case and unbuckled the 3 latches and then turned to me "This cool?". I nodded and she opened the case. She read the card in the case. "This 1962 Gibson SG Sunburst as been authenticated to have been played by Adam Jones of Tool. What the fuck dude are you fucking my asshole dry right now? This was Adam Jones guitar?" I nodded and said "Yeah it was his. Most of undertow was wrote and played with that." Summer was just staring at the guitar and said "Okay dude what the fuck? You gave your clothes away, closed your bank account and now you're giving your 11 year old nephew Adam Jones' fucking guitar? I'm sure he's a great kid but are you for real?" I put the note on top of the guitar and closed the case. Then I stood up and walked out. "Close the door on the way out." I said without looking back. It was starting to get to me. My sister had pictures all over her kitchen and hallways and bookcases and tables. Fucking everywhere. I had to get out of there. I was beginning to have second thoughts. I heard Summer and the box of cereal as I walked out the front door. I went and stood by my Bronco and then heard the front door shut and Summer approaching. "What the fuck was that shit? Are you going to tell me what the fuck is going on?" We just stood there looking at each other for a good 10 seconds. "I'm going to..." I tried to tell her what today was all about. "You're going to what?" She asked. "I'm..." She was just looking at me waiting for me to explain all of this shit we've been doing all day. "I'm going to Neptunes Net." I chickened out. I couldn't do it. "What? What the fuck kind of answer is that?" Summer asked. "It's the only one I got. What do you say? Clam Chowder in a sourdough bowl with a root beer. We can even catch the sunset. You in?" Summer thought for a second and started to get into the Bronco and said "Don't forget to lock your anal sisters door."

CHAPTER 6
NEPTUNES NET & SAND HILL

The drive to Neptunes was quite. Summer mostly messed with the music and telling me random facts about herself. Which was fine with me. I was trying to avoiding talking anyway. Even though I really wanted to. But the thing was I wanted to talk about her, not me. The more she talked the more I wanted to know about her. She had been all over the country and to a lot of other ones. She had a great sense of humor and was obviously educated. When she wasn't angry she was very well spoken. Even her body language and the way she moved her hands when she talked got to me. My desire to know more about this girl was totally fucking up my plan to kill myself.

Once we got there and had our bowls we found a spot on the patio and got situated. We both took a bite at the same time. This was one of my favorite things to eat. So. I figured it would be the perfect last meal. I could tell by her silence that Summer liked it too. "Wow, I can't believe I've never had this." She said. "My uncle Steve used to take us here when we were kids. First we would run up Sand Hill and then come get a bowl." I told her. "Sand Hill, what's that?" Summer asked. "Well it's just like it sounds, a hill of sand. We'll go there after we eat." Aside from a few bullshit comments the rest of the meal was pretty quite. I guess we were both pretty hungry after the day of running around. It only took us about 15 minutes to finish our meal and head out.

We got to the bottom of Sand Hill about 10 minutes after Neptunes. I looked up from the road after we parked. It seemed a lot bigger when I was a kid. But it wasn't the distance that got you, it was the deep sand. It sucked you in with every step, making it almost impossible to get the top. Summer walked up and stood beside me. "So you and you uncle would race up this fucking thing?" She asked. She was looking up at the top of the hill. There was something about the way her blonde dreads and her pink lips reflected the sun. Making them stand out from the rest of her features somehow. She looked like an angel. I snapped out of it when she looked away from the hill and looked towards me catching me staring at her. "Uh yeah, he'd bring me, my brother and my cousin Steven. We'd all race to the top." I told her. "Who'd win?" She asked. "Most of the time uncle Steve won. But every now and then one of us would. We were pretty fast. The sad thing is we stopped coming here when we were about 14. We're all about a year apart. I think we would have had some good battles if we kept coming."

"Why did you stop?" She asked. I took a second to think about it before I answered "I don't know. We just started growing apart in high school I guess, I got into music, my cousin was really into baseball and my brother got all crazy about joining the military. He ended up passing away in Desert Storm when he was 19." Summer reached out and put her hand on my shoulder and said "I'm sorry that happened, what was his name?" That was the first time we had any physical contact and it sent a wave from my shoulder to my toes. I looked at her and didn't realize I was crying until she reached and wiped a tear from my cheek.

I was overwhelmed with emotions and a sense of relief all at the same time. I never talk about my brother, except to my sister. Summer didn't even know me or my brother, why did her sympathy hit me so hard. I don't know but it did. I really missed my brother and it felt good to talk about him. "His name was Eric." I told her. Summer looked me in the eyes and said "No his name IS Eric, not was Eric." Then she pointed to the hill and said "He's still here in a lot of ways." We smiled at each other standing at the bottom of the hill as cars sped by along the coast. "And I'm totally going to beat you just like I'm sure he did." She began to untie her shoes.

    She was serious. What is up with this chick? She knows guitars, Burberry clothes, great music and now she's a athlete too? "You really think you can beat me?" I asked her. She threw her shoes to the side and said "1". I started to take off my shoes. Next she pulled off her socks. I could see her toenails and that they were each painted a different color. "2" she said. She rolled her long dress up around her waist exposing her legs for the first time. Her calves looked like she had been running for years. Was I getting hustled? She got into a take off stance and with a sexy little smile she said "You ready?" I got in my runners stance too. "I think so. Just then she yelled "3!" And we both took off up the hill. She was right by my for about 30 feet or so and then I pulled away. Once I got a good 20 feet ahead of her I stopped to let her catch up. Both of us were out of breath.

    I put my hand out for her to grab and she took it, We walked the rest of the way hand in hand until we reached the top and found the perfect spot to catch the sunset. She pulled a joint out of her hair and a lighter from her pocket. "What else do you got in there?" I asked her reaching towards her hair. "Don't worry about what else I got in there," Summer said while she slapped my hand away. We both laughed a little. She lit the joint and took 4 massive hits. Not even in my best days could I take a hit like that. She didn't even cough. She passed it to me and I did my best. I definitely coughed after my hit but it fine. I took 2 more hits and gave it back to her. Weed was the one thing that I enjoyed. No coffee. No booze. No cigarettes. No pills. None of that shit. Just then it dawned on me that Summer didn't smoke cigarettes, which 1) surprised me and 2) impressed me.

    We sat there quite for about 5 minutes just enjoying the view and then Summer finally asked "So are you going to tell me what today was all about?" I grabbed the joint from her and took a rip before I answered "I'm gonna kill myself." HOLY SHIT did I just say that out loud?!! Summer looked at me and didn't say anything. Maybe she didn't hear me. She took a long drag from the joint and then put her lips to mine and blew the smoke into my mouth. I blew it out and kissed her at the same time. The smoke made a little cloud engulfing our faces. Summer pulled her lips from mine and said "Let's do it together." In a very calm, even tone. "What? Together?" I asked.

    "I'm dead serious." She said with a snicker. Was she fucking with me? Did she think I was joking? "Are you making fun of me right now?" I said as I pulled farther away from her. Summer grabbed my arm and pulled me back towards. "Mike why do you think I have all those pill bottles in my bag?" She asked me. To be honest I had totally forgot about them. Was she for real? Did I meet the perfect chick on the day we BOTH planned to kill ourselves? I had to admit I felt a sense of relief after telling her and saying it out loud. I felt so alone.

    I guess thats the main reason I was going to kill myself in the first place. But now I had a partner. Someone to go on this fucked up journey with. I've always believed that not all relationships were meant to last forever. But 1 day? I mean why else would I met Summer today of all days. Maybe we're supposed to help each other through this. Maybe we're supposed to do this together. Was Summer my Death Angel? Was I hers? Finally I looked her in the eyes and asked "How did you plan to do it?" She opened her bag and pulled out 2 pill bottles and gave them a good shake so I could her the pills inside. "Oxy's". I could see into her purse and all the other pill bottles in there. She had to have at least 13 or 14 bottles.

"What's with all the other bottles you got in there?" Summer started going through her inventory. Pulling out pill bottle after pill bottle. "So these are different kinds of weed. This one is E pills. Oh! This one is Molly, pure Molly, hard to get. This is speed, not really my thing but works when you need it to. These 2 are mushrooms, this one is hash, this one just has rolling papers in it and this one has lighters." I couldn't believe I was driving around with all of this shit today and I told her so "Damn Summer, I can't believe I was driving around with all of this shit today. What if we got pulled over?" Summer just shrugged "I don't know, but we didn't."

I grabbed the joint back from her and took another drag. "I wish I knew you when I was in High School though." I said. She took the joint from me and then said "Why? Were you cooler in high school?" We both laughed at that. I was the first time today that I forgot what I was doing later. Then there was a silence that brought it all back. Not awkward, but, yeah, kinda awkward. Both of our secrets were out. No more hiding what today was really all about. I could tell by Summers smile that she was thinking the same thing. I put a hand on her leg and she rested her head on my shoulder. She passed me the joint and I took a rip. After I let out the smoke I said "I was gonna use a gun."

Summer shot up "Really?" I shouldn't have said that. Why did I? She just stared at me. "What? What's it matter how?" I asked her. "What so violent? A gun? I just don't get it." She said. I could see that it really bothered her. "Too be completely honest I thought it would be quick and painless. I didn't want to hang myself." I told her. "Damn Mike, I just don't get why it has to be so violent. I just think its the wrong way." "Oh I'm sorry, is there's a right way to kill yourself?" I snapped back at her. Was this chick for real? Was she really giving me shit for the way I was going to kill myself? Man, talk about a couple of fucked up people. "I'm not saying its the wrong way or that there even is a right way. But do you really want your sister to have to identify her brothers body with half his head blown off? Because she will."

    She had a point. I didn't really think about after I killed myself. I don't want to put Ashley through that. "You're right. I didn't think of that. So what, Oxy's?" Summer shook her bottle. "I've got plenty." Fuck, Summer really was my Angel of Death. She walked in front of my Bronco and almost gets hit. Now she's helping my kill myself. What the fuck? "Where were you going when I almost hit you?" I asked her. "I was on my way to my moms house to drop this off." Summer pulled an envelope out of her bag. "Just like you did at your sisters." "I don't get it. Why did you get in my truck with me then?" I asked. Summer looked away from me and stared at the sunset before she answered me. "I don't know, it just felt like I was supposed to. Like I wasn't supposed to be alone today." I put my arm around her and pulled her tight. We just sat there and watched the rest of the sunset like that. When it was finished we helped each other up. Our faces were so close to each other. Summer reached up with her hand and touched my forehead and said "We're going to a better place."

    Then she kissed me. We kissed like it was our last kiss we would ever have. The passion was indescribable. I pulled her tight with my arms around her. Knowing that we were going to kill ourselves added a tension I don't think I could put into words. When the kiss was over Summer pulled away and put what was left of the joint into a pill bottle and said "This ones roaches." We both laughed and then walked back down the hill to my bronco. Once we got to the street I grabbed her hand and said "Let's go to your moms and drop off the letter. If we're going to do this then you have to. Where does she live?" Summer didn't say anything for a few seconds and then said "She might be home. I really didn't want her there when I dropped off my suicide note." Yeah could understand that. "Where does she live?" Summer rolled her eyes and said "She's in Huntington?" What? That's right next to my place in Newport. OK, lets go there and if she's home then will we bail. But if she's not we drop off the letter. Deal?"

    Summer thought about it and then said "Alright, but I'm driving." I held out the keys and she snatched them and was in the drivers seat faster than I thought was possible foe her to move. Before I jumped in the passenger seat I had a feeling come over me that didn't make me feel good. It was one thing to kill myself. But now I'm bringing this girl with me? Fucking going to her moms to drop off her suicide note? What the fuck happened to today. I jumped in and Summer sped off much faster then I liked. But fuck it, let her have her fun on our last day. The drive to her moms house was a pretty quite one. Summer didn't even really play the iPod. For the first time today I actually heard a song all the way through. But she did do a lot of touching. Every red light was some form of affection. Holding my hand, rubbing my shoulder. Putting her hand on my thigh. It was like she was trying to get it all out of her system before we killed ourselves. I didn't mind it at all.

CHAPTER 7
SUMMER'S MOMS HOUSE

Summer slowly pulled along side the curb of the house next to her moms and just sat there for a second. It wqs your average Huntington Beach house. It was probably 3 or 4 bedrooms. The lawn was very well kept "Everything ok?" I asked. She took a deep breath and said "Yeah, lets just get in and get the fuck out. I don't want to be here if my mom comes home. It's Tuesday so she's bowling." She got out of the bronco and I followed her across the lawn to the front door. Summer picked up a plant on the porch and grabbed a key. She unlocked the door and we both walked in.

The house was just as nice inside. Very nice furniture. But I could smell the cigarettes. "I'll be right back" Summer said and then walked through the living room and made her way to one of the rooms. "Can I use the bathroom?" I asked as she walked away. "Go through the kitchen and to the right." She yelled back. I went through the kitchen and there was an office the the left and a bathroom on the right. I from the bathroom I could hear Summer moving around the house. I finished pissing, washed my hands and left the bathroom making my way back to the front room. But the fridge caught my eye.

It was full of pictures and I stopped to look them over. I saw one that had to be Summer in high school. She had short purple hair. Another one of her as a little kid, probably about 7. Another one of her but older, her dreads were just starting. There were pictures of her with other people I assumed were her family. One was a Christmas photo. A thanksgiving photo. Then one picture really got my attention. It was Summer in a hospital bed holding a baby. Then I looked some more and saw 2 more pictures of her holding a baby.

Just then Summer walked in the kitchen "Ready?" She asked me. I grabbed the picture off the fridge and asked "Do you have a kid?" Summer took the picture from my hand and put it back on the fridge and walked out of the kitchen to the front door, leaving me alone in the kitchen. "Summer." I called out after her. I followed her out of the house, running to catch her. I grabbed her by the arm and spun her around at the end of the driveway. When she turned around there were tears in her eyes. This time my tone was different when I asked her "Do you have a kid?" Summer looked at the ground and took a deep breath to pull herself together before saying "Her name is Autumn. She's. The state took her away from me from me 3 years ago. I haven't seen her in 2."

    I didn't know what to say. But there was now way I could let her kill herself now. A kid changes everything. "Summer you can't kill yourself. . I had no idea you had a kid." She finally looked up at me with anger in her eyes and said through tears " who the fuck are you to tell me what I can and can't do? You don't know shit about me or what I've been through. All day is been your shit. So don't all of a sudden judge me when you're the one going to blow your head off."

    Summer started walking away. I got in front of her to block her path. " You're right I was, I am. But I'm not leaving a kid behind. No one's depending on me." Summer looked me dead in the eyes and softly said "My daughter hasn't depended on my for 3 years." I put my hands on her shoulders and said "I'm sure you can get her back. But if you kill yourself you'll never know. It can't be the answer." She walked passed me to the bronco and got in on the passenger side. I stood outside of her door. We were at a stalemate. Finally I said "Summer I can't do this with you."

Summer opened the door and jumped out right in front of my face. "FUCK YOU! You don't know a fucking thing about me. Do you want to know why they took her? Do you want to know why I haven't seen her in 2 years? They took her because her dad was molesting her. Do you know how fucking horrible of a mother I had to be for that to happen? How high I had to be that I didn't noticed that? So don't you dare tell me about what she needs. Because she needed me and I wasn't there. I don't deserve her. I never did. The truth is I was pissed when I got pregnant. I was mad I couldn't get high anymore. She's deserves better than me."

Summer broke down and cried. I took her in my arms and held her tight. "Summer you can't do this. What her dad did isn't your fault." She looked up at me and said "I died 3 years ago when they took her from me. This world just hasn't let me go yet and if I don't do it with you tonight, I'm just going to do it some place else. I believed her. She looked tormented by what her ex did to their daughter. And she was right, who the fuck was I to tell her what to do? I was doing the exact same thing. I grabbed her face in both of my hands and pulled her her to my lips and kissed her.

She wrapped her arms around my neck pulling down closer. What started as a peck turned into a full on passionate kiss. We stopped kissing and just held each other and Summer whispered "I just don't want to be here anymore." I pulled away to look at her and answered "Lets go to my house." She nodded and we got into my bronco.Summer put the keys in the ignition but didn't start the bronco. She took her hands off the key and turned to me. "What?" I asked her. "All day we've been running around doing your shit. Goodwill, your bank, your landlord. All your little death errands." I interrupted her "Suicide errands." "What?" She asked me. "You said death errands, but I was calling them suicide errands." Summer rolled her eyes. "Whatever, suicide errands. That's not the point. I got a couple things I want to take care before we go to your apartment." For some reason I had a bad feeling about what summer needed to do before she killed herself. But she did go with me to get my stuff done. "What types of things?" I asked her. "Just gotta talk to a couple people." Was all Summer said. She started up the bronco and pulled away from the curb. I could see a car pull into her moms driveway in my rear view mirror.

CHAPTER 8
THE ROGUE TAVERN

We pulled into the parking lot of a shady dive bar called The Rogue Tavern. Mostly trucks and few Harley's in the parking lot. Summer parked towards the back of the lot. She turned the key and killed the engine and then just sat there looking at the bar. "Are we waiting on something?" I asked. "I'm thinking" Summer said. "About what?" I asked her. "What I'm going to say." Summer whispered. "To who?" Why the fuck did she whisper? I was getting impatient waiting to know what we were doing at this bar. "I doesn't matter. When we go in just go to the bar and order a drink. Max should be there" Summer said and then she got out of the bronco leaving me sitting there. I jumped out and ran to catch up with her. "Who the fuck is Max?" I asked running after her.

"She's the bartender." Summer yelled back at me. "Summer are you gonna tell me what we're doing here?" I asked. She didn't slow down. Just kept walking towards the bar. Then she said "Just order me a White Russian and wait for me." She opened the door and immediately went to the left leaving me standing alone in the doorway. For a second everyone stopped what they were doing and looked at me. Lynyrd Skynyrd was playing, the lights were dim and they definitely didn't care if people smoked here. There was about 10 or 12 people in the whole bar. All guys except the bartender, which I guessed was Max. I started to make my way to the bar but I had to walk past the pool table to get there. There was 5 guys standing around the table all watching me go by. "What's up fellas?" I asked and gave the 'whats up' nod and got just cold stares back. I got to the bar and sat at one of the stool at the corner. "What can I get ya sweetie?" Max was one of those older ladies that you could tell was hot when she was younger. But you could see the years of smoking and drinking had taken their toll on her. She reminded me of Peggy Bundy from Married with children. "I'll take a Jack n Coke and a White Russian please." I told her. "Comin' right up." She said and turned to make our drinks. It just took a couple minutes and Max brought the drinks and set them them down in front of me. "I gotta admit thats an odd combination of drinks for one person" she said. "Oh the Jack n Coke is mine," I told her. "I'm waiting on my friend, she's in the bathroom I think." Max just smiled and said "I hope she's not in our bathroom." Just then Summer walked up and said "Don't worry Max, I didn't sit on the seat." Max looked shocked but extremely happy to see Summer. She almost ran around the bar to greet and hug Summer. "My lord al'mighty girl," Max said "It's been too long. I haven't seen you since you and Steve... well never mind that. It's so good to see you." Then she took Summers face in her hands and kissed her forehead.

    Just then one of the guys from the pool table held up a empty picture and yelled "Max, another one." Max let go of Summer and said "Don't you go anywhere," and then to the guy at the pool table she yelled "Billy don't you fucking yell at me again, you hear me boy." The rest of the guys thought this was pretty funny and laughed at him. Summer sat down next to me. "Oh damn it girl," Max said while she was filling up another picture of beer "White Russian, I should've known it was you and you got yourself a handsome man right there"

    Summer looked at me and put her hand on my leg and said "He's ok." Max went to take the picture of beer to the pool table. Just then one of the guys from the pool table came over and learned on the bar next to me a little too close. He was a skinny kid about 25 years old, probably 140lbs at most and about 5'8 or 5'9. He holing a pool stick in one hand and a cigarette and beer in the other. He's clothes were definitely he's work clothes. He still had on his work boots too. The way he walked up told me I needed to keep an eye on this guy. "Well I'll be, I can't believe my fucking eyes. Summer, I didn't think you'd have the balls to show your face here again." I could feel Summer tensed up. "What do you want Stu?" She asked. "I don't want nothing from you. But I think Logan might." He snapped back at her. Summer looked at me and I took it has a sign that it was time to say something. "Logan is it, my name is Mike. How's it going?" I said as I stuck my hand out to shake. He just ignored me and looked back at Summer and said "I don't know who your new friend here is, but Steve is on his way."

Fuck this dude. I'd had enough of his shit. I stood up and he realized the size difference between us and his tough guy attitude changed real fast. "Listen Logan," I said in a low serious tone, "I think it's time you went back to your pool game." He definitely got the hint. He put his hands up as if to say I don't want any trouble. "It's cool man. I just wanted to say hi to my old pal Summer here." Then he turned and walked back towards the pool table. I sat back down once I thought he was far enough away. "So Logan seems like a nice guy." I said to her. "He's a fucking scumbag drugie" she said "but just to let you know shit might get real in a few minutes when Steve shows up." I just looked at her waiting for the rest of the story, but she just sat there. "What the fuck. Are you gonna tell me who the fuck Steve is and why shits gonna get real when he gets here?" Summer took a deep breath and said "Steve is this guy I was dating for a little while." "That's it? What the fuck? Just tell me whats going on or I'm fucking bailing." I told her. I had shit to do. I should have been laying face down in my shower by now. But instead I'm sitting here in this dirty ass dive bar waiting on Steve. "I stole about 4 grand from Steve," she said "but he was driving my car and got pulled over and it got impounded and the motherfucker wouldn't help me get it out. So I took it." Now I took the deep breath. "So is this the thing you wanted to do before we go to my apartment, deal with Steve?" I asked her. Summer looked at me with murder in her eyes. I knew this wasn't something she took lightly. "I hate this motherfucker," she said in a low scary voice that didn't sound right coming out of someone so pretty. "I can't go to my grave without finishing this."

What did she means by 'finish this'? She definitely wasn't telling me something. "Alright Summer, come clean. Why are we really here?" She looked me right in the eye and said "1968 Chevy Camaro Super Sport." "What the fuck is that?" I asked her. "You gotta be fucking kidding me?! Are you retarded? It's only one of the greatest cars ever made." Just then Max came to check on us. "Are you two ok?" Summer downed her drink in 2 gulps and said "1 more." I still had a full glass so I said "I'm fine, thank you though." Max patted my hand and said "I like this one Summer, he's so polite." "How much do I owe you" I asked her as she started making Summers White Russian. "Don't worry about it sweetie. You just keep this one out of trouble and tip me big the next time you both come on by." I looked at Summer and we both laughed. Goddamn, how morbid. We're laughing because we both knew there wasn't going to be a next time. Life can be pretty disturbing sometimes. "And don't think you're getting out of here without telling me where you've been these past few months. I gotta stock up before the rush comes in," Max said "but I'll be back in a bit and we'll go have a smoke and some good ol' girl talk, ya hear me?" "You bet Max." Summer told her. Once Max was busy again I said to Summer "First off I'm not retarded and second I know what the fuck a 68 Camaro is. I'm what does that have to do with anything?" "Steve drives a tricked out 68' and I'm gonna steal it." Summer said like it was nothing and took a drink of her White Russian. I couldn't tell if she was serious.

    "I'm dead serious too," Summer said as if she could read my mind. "This fucking asshole lied and cheated on me some many fucking times and then he gets my car impounded too? Fuck that dude. No, he's not getting away with it." "But Summer, he didn't get away with it. You took 4 grand from him," I said "Let's just get out of here before this gets out of hand." Summer downed the rest of her drink and slammed the glass on the table and said "No. Fuck Steve. He's not a good person. Some people deserve what they get. He's thinks he's so fucking cool because he's good looking and has that fucking car. No Mike, I'm doing this with or without you." I didn't know what to say. I should have just left. I should have walked right out of the door and then I heard what everyone else in the bar heard. Someone yelled "SUMMER? You fucking bitch!"

CHAPTER 9
STEVE

We both turned our heads to the door of the bar. Steve was standing there with Logan right next to him with this stupid fucking grin on his face. I told myself if it comes to it I'm breaking his fucking teeth. Summer was right, Steve was a handsome dude. He looked just like Daniel Craig, the James Bond dude. He was built too. Shit I hope he didn't train any type of MMA. He could be a problem if he did.

Everyone in the bar was looking at either us or Steve. Some even looked like they were at a tennis match with their heads going back and forth between us. No one moved. Then Steve & Logan started walking towards us. It didn't take long before they were right in front of us. "Where's my fucking money bitch?" I stood up and Steve and I stood eye to eye. He didn't have the same reaction his sidekick had. Steve wasn't a coward like Logan. We stood there for about 6 seconds without a word or movement. He really did look like fucking James Bond.

I had this thought while I was looking into his eyes. It's not a good one but I thought 'I wonder if I could kill this guy'. I've been doing MMA for over 20 years. If there was ever a time to find out if I could kill someone, it was the day I was going to kill myself. No jail time. No repercussions at all. Plus I wanted to see if I had the skills to do it. I knew I could choke him out. But could I punch him to death? With that being my thought process I wasn't worried about fighting Steve or Logan or even both of them. Just then Max came from the back with a case of bottles and put them down and came over to us. "Goddamn it Steve! Not tonight! Take this shit outside you hear me? GO!" Steve didn't budge. Neither did I. Then Steve broke his gaze and turned to look at Summer. "Don't worry Max," he said "I just wanna talk to Summer here" Then he sat in my seat. I had to admit that was a pretty good move. "You Just don't start any shit in my bar you hear me?" Max said. "We hear you Max," Steve answered "we're gonna go outside and talk anyway. Right Summer?" Summer looked at me as if she was asking if I was in or out. I nodded ever so slightly. "Yeah, lets go outside." Summer said. She stood up and Steve grabbed her by the arm to lead her out. I grabbed his hand and took it off her arm then released it and said "She already said we'd go outside. You don't need to touch her." Steve looked at me and laughed before saying "look at Captain Save a Ho here. Just get the fuck outside." I looked down and he had a hand gun pointed at my stomach. He tried to keep the rest of the bar from seeing it but I think they all knew because no one did shit.

"Logan," he said "take Summer outside and I'll escort the Captain here." Logan grabbed Summer by the arm and lead her towards the door. Steve waved the gun in their direction with the tiniest movement. I followed Logan and Summer with Steve behind me. This time I walked pass the pool table no one looked at me. Everyone just kept their heads down, like nothing was happening. Logan pushed Summer through the doors out to the parking lot. The lights were way brighter than the inside of the bar. I followed them outside with Steve and his gun behind me.

Logan walked Summer just around the corner of the bar. Steve pushed me that way with his gun in my back. Once we got out of sight from the parking lot and front entrance he stopped hiding his gun and pointed it at my chest. He moved closer to Summer, now everyone was in front of me. I was waiting for the right moment to knock the gun out of his hand. But he never took his eyes off me. He looked at me the whole time he talked. "So did she tell you what she did to me? He asked me. "Yeah," I said "She told me you got her car impounded so she took the money for her car." Steve and Logan both laughed. "Is that what she told you?" Summer tried to get out of Logans grasp but he held her in place. Steve took the gun off of my and pointed it right at Summers head. "Where the fuck do you think you're going bitch?," Steve asked "Why don't you tell him what else you did." "Fuck you Steve." Summer said. Steve took a deep breath and said "This bitch didn't just take my money. She fed my 4 dogs laxatives. My whole fucking house was covered in dog shit." Summer laughed and he slapped her in the face. I took a step towards him and he swung the gun around back at me. This time it was pointed at my face. "Don't even think about it Romeo" Steve told me. He took a step towards me and I took another step back. I put my hands up thinking with my hands up by my face I would have a better chance of grabbing the gun. His back was to Summer. I looked at her and she mouthed "I'm sorry."

    What was I doing? I was going to kill myself today. I was even going to use a gun. So why the fuck did I care if it was my gun or Steves gun? But if I get shot then what happens to Summer. I don't know why but I started laughing. Louder and louder until Steve finally said "What the fuck is so fucking funny asshole?" I kept laughing. "Shut the fuck up!" he snapped. "I'm its so fucking funny." I said in between laughs. "4 dogs! That must have been so much shit." I said as I continued laughing. Steve didn't like that at all and yelled "I SAID SHUT THE FUCK UP!!". Then Summer said "Steve!", he turned to face her and in that split second with Logan holding her arms Summer lifted her leg and kick him square in the balls. Steve instantly fell to his knees. I jumped at him and grabbed the gun. Logan screamed. But it was a scream that chick would make. Summer got free from him and I pointed the gun at Logans face. "Hey hey hey, lets just chill." He said with his hands in the air. "Shut the fuck up Logan. Just get the fuck out of here." Summer said. Steve was rolling around on the ground moaning in pain. Logan looked at him then back at us and we could see the gears turning in his head. I told him "Logan just go man. Live to fight another day buddy. Just go." Logan looked down at Steve and said "Sorry man, I'm not trying to get shot." And he ran out in the parking lot. He started his truck and sped off out of the parking lot onto the street.

    Steve was starting to get his wits about him again. Trying to get up on one knee. So I gave him a good punch to the head that laid him out. He laid on the ground almost unconscious. Summer got down and started going through his pockets. She grabbed his wallet and keys. She took the money and went to the door of the bar and stuck her head in.

    "Hey. Drinks on me!" And she through the money in the bar. Then she turned to me and said "Let's go" and she started walking to Steves Camaro. "Summer what are doing?" I asked her. She didn't answer me, she just got into his car and started it up. Steve had definitely built that engine up. It was a true muscle car. Summer rolled down the window "Just get in your truck and follow me," she said "and keep up, I'm gonna drive fast." I ran to my bronco and followed her out of the parking lot not know where I was going. We tore out of the parking lot out onto the street.

CHAPTER 10
SAVANNA HIGH SCHOOL

Summer pulled into the parking lot of the school and opened the passenger door of the Camaro. I guess she wanted me to get in. I shut off my bronco and ran over to Steves car and jumped. Summer revved the engine and gave me a sly smile and said "Buckle up buttercup, we're gonna get crazy." Once I snapped the seatbelt she floored the gas pedal and we started doing donuts in the high school parking lot like we were 15. We took turns racing around the parking lot. Doing donuts. Slamming on the brakes to see how far we could slid on the tires seeing who got the longest tire marks. Summer won that contest. But I think my donuts were tighter.

    Then the car ran out of gas and the fun ended just has face as it started. We sat there in the middle of the parking lot and had a good laugh at all the skid marks in the parking lot. It looked like a giant art project or like crop circles. "So what now?" I asked her. "What do you mean? Summer asked back. "What are we gonna do with the car?" I asked. Summer laughed and said "Nothing." I was confused and she could see it. "What don't you understand?" She asked. "Well we can't just leave it here." I said. Summer laughed again "Why not?," she asked "I don't give a fuck what happens to it. Fuck Steve. I'm just gonna leave to the keys on the seat and be done with it." She was right why not? We were going to kill ourselves tonight. Why should we give 2 fucks about Steves car.

    We got out of the Camaro and started walking to my bronco and Summer stopped, gave something a thought and ran back to the car. "Summer what are you doing?" I yelled at her. "Just give me a sec." She yelled back. She went to the and grabbed the keys and ran around to the trunk and popped it up and dug around and the slammed the trunk back down with authority. She had a couple rags in her hand. She ran to the drivers side and sat down in the seat. I couldn't see her but my guess was she was taking a dump in Steves car. After a few minutes she popped up and fixed her underwear and ran back to where I was standing. "Took a shit? I asked her. "I tried but the chamber was empty. I just took a pretty good size piss." We both laughed and got into the bronco. I stared the engine and then turned to looked at Summer. I had so much fun with her. I don't know if I was ready to go back to my apartment. I knew once we were there it was all going to end. As if Summer read my mind she leaned over and gave me a kiss and whispered "Let's go to you place."

CHAPTER 11
MY APARTMENT

We walked in and Summer looked around the apartment, scanning the place. I wonder if she was thinking 'Is this where I'm spending my last minutes on earth?' Then she said "You have some really cool art." "Thanks" I said. Summer took her jacket off and put it over the back of the couch then she sat down and patted the seat next to her telling me to come sit by her. I went and sat next to her. "So what do you we do now?" She asked. "I guess we take the Oxy's right?" Summer looked shocked that I said that. "Just like that? Just kill ourselves?" Summer said. "Well shit Summer, then what?" I asked. "How about some music, a glass of wine, a fucking bong rip or something. This is fucking Romeo and Juliette man. Fucking Thelma and Louise." She had a point. "Wait, am I Louise?"

I asked. We both laughed. "You know what I mean." She said. "You're right, the stereo is right there. Go put on some music and I'll get us some drinks." I told her as I got up and headed to the kitchen. About a minute later as I was pouring our drinks Talking Heads- This Must Be The Place came on. I loved that song. In fact it was one of my favorites. The fact that she picked that of all the songs she could have picked gave me goosebumps. She walked over to me in the kitchen and gave me a Kidd on the cheek and asked "where's the bathroom?" I pointed to the end of the hall. She walked to the bathroom and I never took my eyes off her. She got to the doorway and stopped before she walked in.

I Knew instantly what she was looking at. She looked back down the hallway towards me. "Come here." she said. I walked down the hallway to the bathroom and stopped in the same spot she had. We both looked at the .45 on the bathroom counter. Summer looked at me in the mirror and asked "Is this where you were going to do it?"

I opened the shower curtain and said "Right in there. I was going to turn on the shower to hopefully help with the sound and the mess." Summer put her hand on mine and we both closed the curtain and said "That's not how anymore." There was something in the way she looked at me. I leaned in to kiss her and she pulled me I the rest of the way. I picked her up and sat her on the countertop. Her legs wrapped around my waist. We pulled each others clothes off completely In tune with each other. No awkward movements.

   Not like it was our first time together, but like it was our 100th time we had done this. The next the I knew we were having sex. It was hard not to think about this being the last time I was going to fuck or make love or hug or kiss.It added to it in some morbid way. It made it more passionate. Summer turned around so I could take her from behind In front of the mirror. Once that happened it didn't take long for me to finish. That view in the mirror was all it took. Summer turned back around and kissed me and then said "Can I get that glass of wine now?" "Of course." I pull my boxers on while Summer put my shirt on. She looked so fucking in my button up.

   I walked to the kitchen and grabbed her glass of wine from the countertop and then I heard it. A gun shot. I almost didn't believe it.I though for a split second that it was the music. But it wasn't. I knew that second that I had lost her. The one thing that made today ok was dead in my bathroom. I ran out of the kitchen and into the hallway and stopped. I could see feet in the doorway. I slowly walked towards the bathroom. As I got closer I saw that she was sitting on the toilet. Blood covered the wall behind her, with thick pieces of brain and skull and hair. There was literally 2 of her dreads stuck the wall. She just sat there on the toilet, she was on the verge off slipping off the seat.

A huge hole was on the top of her head. Which made the look on her face that must more crazy. She actually looked peaceful. The gun was on the floor next to her. I just didn't understand it. Why the fuck couldn't you wait Summer? What the fuck happened to us taking Oxy's? I reached down and picked the .45 up off the floor. I looked at myself in the mirror, then back down at Summer. I went back into the living room and started the song over. This Must Be The Place. How fucking poetic. I actually laughed out loud to myself. This definitely was the place I thought. I went back into the bathroom and knelt down in front of Summer. I straightened her up on the toilet and gave her one last kiss. I stood up and looked into the mirror. For some reason I started laughing, almost to the point of tears. The barrel was still warm when it touched my lips.

Acknowledgements:

I want to thank anyone that bought this book. You taking a chance on my book means the world to me. Your support is a huge motivation to me. Thank you.

I also want to thank my grandpa, George J. Dutra for always believing in me and telling me "You can do it."

Made in United States
North Haven, CT
30 November 2024